LONG SPIKES

LONG SPIKES

A STORY BY
JIM ARNOSKY

CLARION BOOKS
NEW YORK

Clarion Books
a Houghton Mifflin Company imprint
215 Park Avenue South, New York, NY 10003
Text and illustrations copyright © 1992 by Jim Arnosky

Library of Congress Cataloging-in-Publication Data

Arnosky, Jim.
Long Spikes : a story / by Jim Arnosky.
p. cm.
Summary: Long Spikes, a deer who is orphaned as a yearling when his mother is
killed, grows to maturity and displaces the old one-eyed buck from his position as
dominant male.
ISBN 0-395-58830-8
1. Deer—Juvenile fiction. [1. Deer—Fiction.] I. Title.
PZ10.3.A86923Lo 1992 91-3849
[Fic]—dc20 CIP AC

VB 10 9 8 7 6 5

This book is dedicated to
DR. LEONARD LEE RUE III,
our foremost authority
on white-tailed deer

CHAPTER ONE

*O*n a cold and icy morning in the middle of March, three deer—a doe and her twin fawns—were making their way in single file down a wooded hillside. The leaf litter on the ground was coated with frost and the frozen earth beneath was rock hard. It was slippery going, even for the surefooted deer, and they progressed slowly.

The sky was overcast and gray, but clearing rapidly. A single shaft of morning sunlight shining through the clouds played softly on the doe's long neck and broad side. Her coat of blue-gray hair had the typical markings of white-tailed deer—a half moon of white under each eye, a band of buff-white across the snout, white on chin and belly. The whitest of white hair was on the underside of the deer's dark brown tail, out of sight. When it was time to flee from danger, the tail, raised high, became a waving white flag for her fawns to follow.

The fawns—a buck and a doe—were eleven months old and only slightly smaller than their mother. The young buck had two fuzzy, button-like bumps on his forehead where his first year's antlers were beginning to grow.

The big doe was pregnant again, carrying a new set of twin fawns inside her. As she led her family down the slippery trail, the mother doe was very much on guard for any sign of danger. Every few yards she paused, swiveling her ears to listen in different directions. She raised her nose and sampled scents carried to her by light breezes. She glanced around to check the woods for threatening movements. Only when she was completely satisfied that all was safe did she continue down the trail.

A single crow flying over the hilltop called "Caw-caw," "all's well" in crow, to the flock of hundreds of other crows congregated out of sight somewhere in the surrounding forest. The deer on the hillside did not look up at the crow calling overhead. But as the big black bird's flight brought it more in line with their line of sight, all three deer saw the crow flap eastward over the shaded meadow below, still covered with snow. "Caw-caw," the crow called out again as it wheeled slowly in the sky, turning due south to follow the line of river that flowed by the snowy field.

The young buck stopped, halting his sister behind him, and stared into the distance, tracking the black speck of crow in the sky. The young doe, seeing how far their mother had moved on, became impatient to catch up, and nudged her brother's rump with her snout to urge him to get going.

Farther up the heavily wooded hill and downwind from the deer, three silent, shadowy forms blended with the trees. Coyotes, a large female and her two slightly smaller offspring, were watching the deer's slow progression. During winter, the three coyotes had killed a weak and starving deer—easy prey. They had also fed on a deer carcass they had found frozen solid in a mound of snow. The three deer moving down the hillside were obviously healthy. Under normal circumstances they could outrun, outmaneuver, and escape a coyote attack. The coyotes on the hilltop knew there was little chance of catching and killing them. But it had been days since the coyotes had full bellies. They were hungry, and the deer scent wafting uphill made their mouths water.

While the younger coyotes paced back and forth behind her, the mother coyote sat back on her haunches, fixing her large yellow eyes on the big doe leading the way ever so slowly down the trail. When the doe's right hind hoof slid on a patch of ice, causing her momentarily to lose her balance, the old coyote's legs all flinched as if to run. She licked out her long tongue and moistened her nose, better to collect the delectable deer scent, then licked her chops, revealing two long white upper fangs. The left fang, pushed inward by a blow long ago, was hooked back more sharply than the one on the right. The coyote licked her chops again. A stronger uphill breeze ruffled the long gray fur on her chest. She luxuriated in the aroma it carried, and kept her eyes glued to the doe.

Halfway down the hill, the doe slowed up even

more to negotiate another slippery ice patch. She stepped along carefully, using the sharp edges of her hooves to break a path. The young buck and doe took the opportunity to pause and nibble tender leaf buds from trailside saplings. Suddenly their mother slipped again. This time she slid off the trail and tumbled violently down the steep slope. Instantly the watching coyote sprang, running down the hill. The two younger coyotes took off after her.

The doe, still sliding on her side, kicked and scrambled, trying to get up. From above, her fawns watched cautiously. In the corner of his vision the young buck spotted the big coyote racing down the hill, and he bolted off the icy trail and uphill through the woods, his tail raised high in alarm. The young doe had not seen the coyote, but she panicked and ran also, following the bouncing white flag of her fleeing twin.

The coyotes sped toward the big doe, who was still struggling to stand. Regaining her footing at last, she saw the largest coyote less than fifty feet away and coming. She snorted and dashed off down the hillside, her hooves chopping through the frozen leaf litter. She kept her tail clamped down tight. There was no use flagging her fawns. And instinctively she knew that if she raised her tail, the bright white flag would only help her pursuers chase her.

At the bottom of the hill was an old stone wall. The doe was forced to slow down to step over strewn and partially piled boulders. Then she ran out of the woods onto the broad meadow, where the ground was soft and wet beneath six inches of sugary snow. The doe picked up speed. She was charging headlong for the river, many hundred yards away, where she could lose the coyotes and swim to safety.

The mother coyote leaped the tumbled stone wall well ahead of her offspring, and ran a wide half circle over the field to head the deer off. The two younger coyotes were still far behind when their mother finally caught up with the doe on the field's far side, one hundred yards from the river. Hoof and paw marks overprinted in the snow as the coyote galloped along right beside the

running deer. Their sides rubbed and bumped together as the coyote lunged repeatedly, jaws snapping, trying to catch hold of the doe's coat.

The doe ran onward toward the river, now just fifty yards away. The coyote dogged her, nipping at her legs and side. Then, lunging upward, the coyote sunk her sharp fangs into the doe's long neck. The shock of the wound and the weight of the coyote hanging on her neck halted the doe in her tracks. She came to a sliding stop, her front legs spread wide apart, her hooves dug down in the snow.

With the aid of her hooked fang, the coyote kept her hold on the doe, even when the powerful deer began bucking and lurching forward, trying desperately to reach the river.

The doe splayed all four cloven hooves for better traction and to keep from falling over as she plodded ahead, exhausted. The coyote hung on as her prey moved down the gently sloping field to a spot twenty yards from the river where, finally, her teeth severed a main artery in the deer's neck. A stream of hot red blood spurted out onto the cold white snow.

The two young coyotes reached the scene simultaneously and attacked the wounded deer, bringing her down on her side. Her steaming overheated body sank into and melted the snow. With all three coyotes on her, the deer managed to get to her feet once more. But she had lost a lot of blood, and she collapsed again, weak and helpless on the snow. Her vision blurred and faded. For a few moments, through the coyotes' snarls and growls, the doe heard the river running by. Then she died.

The sentinel crow, flying high above the meadow, spotted the fresh blood on the snow and saw the coyotes feeding on the deer. The crow called excitedly, "Ca-caw-caw-caw." Circling lower, it called out again, "Ca-caw-caw-caw," arousing the hidden flock. Within minutes the sky was speckled with hundreds of crows, all circling, flapping, cawing loudly in the air above the white meadow. Then the flock descended and swarmed around the coyotes, trying to drive them away from their kill.

The coyotes had eaten only entrails and one fawn fetus. They snapped fiercely at the crows and fought for position on the carcass. The mother coyote pushed through the black birds, took a stabbing crow beak in the cheek, hooked her teeth into the second fawn fetus, and ran off with it. Her offspring ran after her, with something of the deer clamped tightly in each of their mouths.

The horde of crows fed on the deer noisily, in competing gangs, snatching morsels of warm entrails, tearing bits of body hair and flesh, and picking at the eyes and face.

Up on the wooded hillside the young buck and doe had circled back to the trail, expecting to rejoin their mother. Now they were standing close together, anxious and alert, watching and listening to the commotion below. The scents drifting up to them from the meadow were muddled and confusing. They did not know what had happened; they knew only that their mother was not with them. They felt anxious and unsettled. The young doe nervously stomped a forefoot. The buck looked at his sister, then back down toward the field.

A chickadee flew by and alighted on a twig just inches above the buck's nose. The deer watched closely as the tiny bird straightened a few feathers in a folded wing, then flew farther down the trail. The young buck followed the bird. The doe followed her twin. Together they walked away, leaving the noisy crows behind them.

CHAPTER TWO

*A*ll their young lives the fawns had followed their mother to feeding areas, to drinking spots, to hiding places. In winter they had followed her to the evergreen forest where, sheltered from the wind, they and many other families of deer tramped a maze of trails in the deep snow as they fed. And when winter was ending, the young buck and doe had followed her out of the evergreen forest to the wooded hillside. Now, for the first time, they were on their own. They were not lost. Deer can never be lost within their home range. But they were unsure of where to go next.

They followed the trail down the wooded hillside and wandered into a dense cedar bog, where they bedded close together on a hummock for the remainder of the day.

At sunset the orphans left the bog and, picking up another narrow trail, found their way to a bend

in the river. The two then followed the river
downstream, walking in the cover of giant cot-
tonwood trees growing along the riverbank.

A little over half a mile downstream, they came
to a narrow brook, one of the river's many spring-
fed feeder streams. The brook trickled through a
deeply eroded channel in the riverbank, poured
off a ledge of rock, and spilled its sparkling water
into the greater stream. The deer lingered, drawn
to the tiny stream. Something about it was vaguely
familiar.

The doe stood beside the brook looking at the colorful stream-bed pebbles and listening to the happy sounds of the running water. The buck walked along the snow-covered bank and attempted to follow the brook upstream. But his way was blocked by the tangled stems and branches of brush and shrubby trees. He stopped to browse.

The doe took a step into the brook and found the water very cold but only inches deep. She pressed down with her submerged hoof and felt that the gravel bed was firm. Then she stepped in with all four hooves and began walking in the water. The buck, munching a wad of soft bark and green buds, saw his sister moving up the brook. He hopped over a small shrub and ran splashing into the shallow stream to catch up with her.

As they traced the brook upstream, the surrounding brush became gradually less dense. Soon they were able to leave the waterway and travel more silently on the bank. Their wet hooves sank through the remaining snow and pressed heart-shaped prints into the mud beneath.

The farther up the brook the two deer walked, the more familiar the terrain seemed. And when at nightfall they entered a great alder thicket surrounded by dark forested hills, a rush of recognition filled their senses as they responded to the tall dry grass, the low brush, the rank odor of wet soil, and the great dome of open sky. Though the deer could not fully comprehend it, somewhere in the thicket, on a dry and grassy spot beside a large willow tree, they had been born nearly one year before.

The joy of homecoming completely overwhelmed the young buck. He hopped high, kicking the night air with his hind legs and sending a spattering of snow and black mud flying off his hooves. The doe simply stood, head held high, smelling, listening, looking, totally absorbing the environment.

For a few weeks it was as if the thicket had been created especially for the young buck and doe. They lived virtually undisturbed. Each night, from dusk to dawn, they fed on leaf buds and tender shoots from the branches of alder, willow, and young red maple trees. Sometimes they would venture into the surrounding woods to hunt for early spring mushrooms and eat the green leaves of wild strawberry and arbutus plants. Mostly they stayed in the heart of the thicket, following the tiny brook, walking its soft banks, going upstream or down to different feeding spots. And every day the deer bedded in the sunlight beside the running water. It was a peaceful quiet place.

One balmy April afternoon, the spring peepers that had been hibernating in the mushy ground throughout the thicket awoke and began to peep. Soon hundreds of the tiny tree frogs were all singing out together, building to a great crescendo of peeping calls that resonated through the warm air. The sound pierced the deer's highly sensitive ears. The doe, alarmed, hopped up to her feet and glanced warily around the thicket. She stomped a hind foot, then a forefoot, to alert the buck. But he just flattened his head down on the ground, wincing at the peeper's loud sounds. As the singing continued, the doe suddenly relaxed. Some connection in her subconscious was made. The sound was harmless. She stepped across the brook and walked away to find a quieter place to rest.

The young buck nestled more tightly on his bed. He rested his white chin on the dry grass and closed his eyes to sleep. A few peepers were still peeping. The brook babbled softly. Suddenly the buck heard a splash, then Splash! Splash! Splash! He popped awake and saw a mink hopping down the center of the brook. The mink was small and sleek. His fur was wet from hunting in the water for fish and crayfish.

The brook was the mink's feeding ground. He knew every inch of its bed and banks from hunting thoroughly one stretch of water a week at a time. Now, after weeks upstream, the mink was concentrating on the section of the brook that ran through the thicket. He did not notice the deer lying just ten feet away.

The mink hopped a few more yards down the center of the stream, then quickly plunged into the water and dug in the mud until he emerged with a crayfish clamped in his mouth. He jumped up onto the stream bank and gobbled up his catch.

The young buck listened intently to the sounds of crayfish shell being crunched and chewed. As soon as the mink finished eating, he ran off over ground, crackling dry leaves and grasses with his small thumping jumps. The buck watched the mink disappear behind a clump of alder stems, and then, with the sounds of the brook and a small chorus of peepers still singing, the deer again rested his chin on the grass and went back to sleep.

With each new spring day the thicket became noisier. Wood frogs, cricket frogs, and carpenter frogs added their individual mating calls to the background music of the peepers. Pairs of blackbirds, sparrows, and warblers built their nests in the grasses and brush and filled the air with their melodious songs.

More and different animals came into the thicket. A small flock of mallards, mostly drakes, dropped in on the brook and stayed. A female red fox, all scraggly looking from being picked and pulled at by nursing pups, hunted in the thicket morning, noon, and night. She was keeping herself fed and bringing freshly killed prey to her pups, to wean them off her milk. The mother fox's disheveled fur made her look much bigger than she was. Though she posed no threat to the deer, they were startled every time they spotted her— especially the young doe, who was by nature more protective than her brother. Every new arrival in the thicket increased her nervousness. She was on guard day and night. Her ears were constantly twitching and swiveling, picking up the slightest sounds—a waddling porcupine's quill-covered tail scraping on the ground, raccoon hands feeling around for crayfish in the brook, or spotted turtles plopping into the water.

The young buck was more relaxed, carefree, and curious about each new animal in the thicket. He paid little heed to his sister's constantly cautioning snorts and foot stomps.

Then, one moonless night, while the deer were feeding near the brook, the doe suddenly picked up a most alarming scent in the cool night air. She stomped once exceptionally hard on the ground, sending a vibration of her anxiety to her brother. The buck stopped feeding and looked up. Immediately he too caught the scent and became as anxious as his twin.

Less than seventy-five feet away, a large male bobcat was padding through the dense brush, hunting for hare. The bobcat moved slowly and silently, carefully placing its soft cushioned paws on the ground, all the while scrutinizing every shadowy clump of vegetation for the shining eyes of his prey.

To stay downwind and out of sight of the bobcat, the deer kept moving in the darkness. They made no sounds, not even to communicate to each other. Instinct told them that such a large predator was a threat. Both deer reacted to the bobcat's presence as though they were being hunted. At one point, as the deer maneuvered through the thicket, they were forced to leave the cover of the alders and pass through an open area. The doe went first. When she had made it safely to cover on the other side, the buck crossed, stepping in his sister's hoofprints. The second he was once again in the cover of the brushy alders, the buck spotted the slinking black silhouette of the bobcat some distance away. The eerie sight, combined with the strong bobcat scent, made hairs on the young buck's neck and back stand on end.

For the remainder of the night, the deer managed to avoid the prowling cat. Though they were hungry, they did not dare to feed. Even after the bobcat, unable to find and kill a hare, had given up and left the thicket, the deer remained edgy, reacting to its lingering scent.

In the morning, as the rising sun gradually illuminated the thicket and breezes whisked away the remaining scent of bobcat, the shadowy fear that had held the deer so firmly all through the night released its grip. Instead of bedding, the young buck and doe stayed up to feed. Then, their hunger assuaged, the deer played a game of chase around the alders, running off the remaining tension of the night-long ordeal.

CHAPTER THREE

*W*ith May came gentle soaking rains. In the thicket, on the knolls, straight green grass blades lanced upward through the tangled mats of dry grass. Beneath the alders, bloodroot bloomed, and tightly furled ferns poked through the leaf litter. In the mud along the brook, fuzzy green fists of hellebore punched out of the wet ground and spread their large leaves to the sun. Higher up on the stream banks, trout lilies blossomed, each yellow flower head bowed downward to the earth. Every tree and shrub branch erupted into leaf. The tiny new leaves turned the thicket and surrounding woods from April's drab tans and browns to pastel shades of yellow and green.

The buck and doe, now yearlings, were gradually losing their blue-gray winter coats of long, hollow insulating hairs as their red-brown summer coats, shorter haired but denser and more luxurious, grew in. The two knobs on the buck's forehead had swelled, and each had grown an inch. The soft, velvety tissue covering, filled with many small blood vessels, nourished the antlers growing inside. Because the velvet's outer hairs were so sensitive, the buck could feel the antlers on his forehead and was aware of how long they were, even though he could not see them. Inside the velvet the developing antler spikes were very soft. Even a slight blow could damage and deform them. Instinctively the buck knew this and was careful not to bump or scrape the velvet. He threaded his way slowly through the thicket, tilting his head, holding his antlers sideways when passing beneath low branches.

Whenever the yearlings walked through areas of dense vegetation, the buck's slow and deliberate movements to protect his antlers caused him to lag far behind his sister. After a while he became accustomed to being by himself. He made no attempt to find the doe. It was always she who came back looking for her twin. Her herding instinct was much stronger than her brother's. She was used to watching out not only for herself, but for him also. Being alone made her nervous. She needed to be with her own kind.

Many small groups of deer were living in the surrounding woods and hollows. So far none of these deer had come into the thicket, and the twins did not venture out. The doe was reluctant to go into the woods alone, and the buck was perfectly content staying where he was. Besides, both deer had come to know the thicket better than any other place they had been. They knew every rise and dip in the land, where the ground was hard and dry and where it was marshy. The yearlings knew every deadfall and how high off the ground each was, so that even in the dark they could leap the prone tree trunks while running at full speed. The buck and doe knew where to find sweet-smelling herbs and pungent mushrooms, and where the soil contained salt and other minerals they craved. The thicket was their home.

One evening in the twilight, a lone male beaver, following the brook downstream, came into the thicket. Where the brook was too shallow for the portly beaver to swim, he ambled along on the stream bottom, climbing over large stones and fallen logs. Wherever he could, he walked out on the brook's bank, his flat feet pressing clear and perfect prints into the wet sand and mud. The prints showed the long separated toes of his rather small forefeet and the wide webs of skin between the toes on his large hind feet. The beaver himself was of medium size, weighing about twenty-five pounds. His thick oily fur was light cinnamon brown. His wide, flat, furless tail was covered with hundreds of small leathery scales of skin. The beaver's eyes were small black beads, visible only when he shifted them and they caught a shine of light.

Every dozen or so steps, the beaver stopped to survey his surroundings. Superbly built for swimming and poorly made for walking or running, he felt uncomfortable on the bank near so shallow a stream. Without deep water to plunge into, he was vulnerable to attack from large predators like coyote, bobcat, and bear. The beaver looked for any movement in the shadowy brush. He stood up on his haunches and sniffed for scents of danger in the air. When he felt secure that danger was not near, he continued his downstream journey.

He had been traveling for many weeks. The beaver pond where he was born was far upstream. As is the way with beavers, as soon as he turned two years old, his parents chased him out to make room in the lodge for new beavers to be born.

When the beaver had reached a point near the center of the thicket where the stream bed was more mud than stones, he slid back into the water and sloshed around, stirring up the soft bottom. Then, using his front feet, the beaver dredged up the loosened mud, carried it to a spot on the bank, and piled it on a clump of grass growing there. The heavy, wet mud flattened down the grass blades and dripped brown water down the bank. The beaver dredged up another load of mud and piled it on the same spot, building the mound a little higher. Again he scraped up mud, this time from the bank. He carried the fresh mud close to his chest and dumped it all on the mound.

A few stars began to twinkle in the sky. The

beaver worked steadily on his mound, adding more mud and occasionally some cut grasses, carefully building the pile into a conspicuous cone. By the time he was finished, the sky was deep indigo and filled with twinkling stars.

In the dark, the beaver moved slowly over the mound, depositing a sweet-smelling oily fluid from two large scent glands located in his hind end. Once the mud was permeated with the beaver's oil, the mound was complete—a scented signpost intended to attract a beaver mate. Having completed his task, the beaver went on a little farther down the stream to fill his growling belly with alder bark. The fresh mud "patty" was left to chance. The beaver had been leaving such scented patties here and there on the brook bank all along his journey, and he was still alone.

Even though the stars were out in numbers, absence of moonlight made the thicket a dark and shadowy place. The yearling deer were walking in the shadows through the alders near the stream. The doe led the way. As had become usual, the buck lagged far behind, walking very slowly, dipping and turning his head to keep his antlers away from poking twigs. The doe weaved through the alders, crossed the brook, and went directly to a weedy knoll on the other side. When the buck came to the brook, he paused to drink. As he sipped the moving water, an evening breeze carrying an odd, sweet scent wafted by his nose. He raised his head from the stream, and with his mouth still dripping water, he turned off the doe's trail and moved upwind to explore the strange new smell.

The deer walked upstream and upwind, along the brook's soft bank. A constant scritching sound was coming from somewhere close by. The buck stopped and listened. It was like the sound of a hare gnawing soft bark, which was familiar to him. The scritching of sharp teeth gnawing wood always made the buck's ears twitch. His ears were involuntarily twitching now as he concentrated once again on the strange new smell and finally located its source—the fresh mud patty on the streambank grass.

The buck nosed the mound and inhaled its full

aroma. It was different from any other smell he had experienced—at once pleasing and intriguing. He nibbled a blade of grass which was sticking up out of the patty. It tasted oily. The longer the buck stood over the mud patty, the more familiar the oily smell became, and the less the young deer's mind was focused on it. Suddenly he was more conscious of the scritch, scritch, scritching sound. He stepped over the mound and stalked upstream along the brushy bank in the direction of the noise until he spotted the beaver feeding on a twig. The deer froze in his tracks, and was spellbound, all eyes and ears and nostrils.

Everything about the beaver was fresh and new. It was big but not threatening. Its teeth were large and formidable, but the sound they made gnawing on the wood was safe and familiar. And the beaver's scent was sweet, much like that of the alluring mud patty the deer had just discovered.

From his hiding place behind the brush, the deer watched curiously as the beaver chewed and cut another alder twig, then held it horizontally with his front paws and gnawed away the bark.

The deer knew the tangy taste of alder bark, and the woody fragrance of it made him lick his nose hungrily. When the beaver had eaten all the alder bark and with it the thin layer of living wood growing just beneath, he dropped the bare white twig on the bank and cut another twig to gnaw. The young buck, mesmerized by the beaver, watched him cut and gnaw twig after twig, until the dark stream bank around the beaver's haunches was littered with white sticks.

After standing stock-still for so long, the deer shifted his body to ease the weight on his legs. In doing so he took a tiny step onto some dry leaves. The crackling noise alerted the beaver, who stopped gnawing and looked up. He could not see the deer hidden behind the brush. The beaver stood up taller on his haunches and sniffed the air, trying to catch a telling scent. But the deer was downwind and the beaver could not smell him. The beaver remained alert, staring toward the deer, and the uncomfortable feeling of being watched overcame the buck. He lowered his head, turned, and slowly slunk away. The beaver saw the movement in the brush and plunged into the stream, where he hid under a clump of vegetation growing out over the water.

The doe, still feeding on the weedy knoll, had become increasingly nervous. She had heard the scritch, scritch of the beaver gnawing as a distant, echoing sound. Not knowing what it was worried her, and now that it had stopped, it worried her all the more. She stood alert, glancing all around, cupping her long ears this way, that way, listening for the scritching to begin again. She was just about to leave and seek her brother when he showed up on the knoll beside her. His stealthful approach and sudden appearance gave her a start, then just as quickly calmed her. She was so glad to have his company, she showed her joy by prancing near him, gently nudging her face against his. And when the buck began to graze, the doe continued to engage him by teasing, muzzling in to steal the very grass he was trying to eat.

Gradually the stars in the sky became obscured by clouds. A raindrop splattered on a leaf the buck was reaching for. Another drop hit his nose. Then there was a downpour. The buck left the knoll and took shelter under the boughs of a streamside pine—one of the few evergreen trees growing in the thicket. The doe, dripping wet, sidled in beside her twin. Together they stood watching and listening to the rain.

The shower was brief. As the sun's first bright rays peered over the horizon, the sky was already clearing. The air smelled scrubbed and perfumed. The thicket birds began the new day singing. The buck and doe folded their long legs under them and bedded down beneath the pine, beside the rain-swollen brook.

The sun was high, directly overhead, when another beaver moseyed into the thicket. It was a female, very dark in color. Like the male, she was a two-year-old who recently had been expelled from her place of birth. Her family lived in a bankside lodge by the river. She had been wandering along the river for a little over a week when she discovered the tiny feeder stream and followed it inland. As soon as she had entered the sunny thicket, she caught wind of the musky scent drifting from the fresh mud mound. Tense with excitement over the prospect of being again with her kind, she followed her nose and the tiny brook directly to the patty, and from there it was an easy search to locate the bachelor male.

When the two beavers met, they accepted each other with much nuzzling and touching and soft murmuring. Immediately afterward the pair set about establishing the thicket brook as their new home. Separately, they began cutting tall grasses and weeds from the banks and, using mud clawed up from the stream bottom, anchored all the clumps of vegetation in the brook bed. In less than an hour the beavers had formed a line of mud and greens bowed slightly upstream against the strong flow—a solid beginning of a dam. Then the beavers each began cutting larger, woodier stems and felling saplings to add bulk to their construction.

All day long the deer heard wood being gnawed and little trees falling. When the sound was nearby, the doe and buck looked searchingly through the brush to locate its source, and then watched curiously every move the busy beaver made. At sunset the deer arose and walked far upstream to find a quiet place to feed.

The beaver pair continued working through the night, adding branches, sticks, mud, and stones to their new dam. By midnight the dam was holding water. By dawn, enough water had been backed up to form a tiny pool. And when the pool was wide and deep enough for the beavers to swim in, they concentrated their efforts on cutting and felling only trees and brush that were in the water.

In the morning, when the sun rose over the thicket, it shone on something new—a small oval of still water, shimmering, reflecting, shining sunlight back.

CHAPTER FOUR

*N*ight after night, and often during daylight as well, the beavers worked, in-
creasing the height and length of their dam.
More and more water was backed up. Inch by inch
the thicket became a pond, and the brook a deep
channel running through it. By the second week
of summer, the trees and brush that lined the
brook's banks were standing in four feet of water.

The deer continued to feed where they could
within the flooded thicket and bedded on the high
ground around the edges of the pond. Even after
they were forced by the flooding to range deeper
into the woods to graze and browse in small clear-
ings, the twins were reluctant to leave the thicket
for good. They returned each morning to the pond
to drink and rest. The buck liked lying on a par-
ticular knoll overlooking the water, where he
could watch the beavers working on their dam,

spot trout jumping after insects, and observe wood ducks and mallards swimming between and around the flooded alder stems. Everything that happened on the pond intrigued him.

Late one afternoon mayflies began emerging from the water in such great numbers that the air above the pond became crowded with the fluttering flies. When one of the delicate insects flew near and alighted on the buck's side, the deer was entranced. He watched the tiny transparent creature as though nothing else existed.

His sister paid little attention to the mayflies or the pond. She lay on her bed and faced the woods. Unlike her more carefree twin, she was ever ready for the possibility of danger. And intuition told her that, if danger came, it would not come from the lively creatures on the pond. It would come on quiet footsteps through the woods.

The doe, totally absorbed in the silent wooded hillside, was startled when suddenly her brother rose and stretched. The sun was going down. It was time to feed. The buck reached down and nosed his sister. She stood and stretched, and together the deer walked down to drink from the pond.

The thicket clearing was awash in apricot-colored light from the setting sun. The surface of the beaver pond reflected the reddened sky. The buck and doe stepped side by side right into the water up to their dewclaws. The doe drank first, and quickly left to nibble greens along the shore. The buck lingered. He drank a little, then lifted his head to look around the pond. A swallow sped by and dipped down to the water to snatch a sip. As the buck bent down to drink again, he noticed his own reflection in the glassy pond. His antlers, still in velvet and now each five inches long, looked like two huge limbless trees silhouetted against the sky. Each velveted antler culminated in a bulbous knob that shone softly. The buck very slowly cocked his head from left to right and watched enthralled as his reflection did the same. He dipped to drink again and with the water, sipped in a floating wad of green algae. He chewed the algae up.

Across the pond, on the opposite shore, a twig

cracked. The young buck snapped up alert and spotted a strange deer also drinking from the pond. It was a bigger buck with a large rack of velvety antlers, each main beam already reaching out beyond the deer's long ears and beginning to branch to five knobby tines.

The older buck finished drinking and looked up across the water at the yearling. Something about the big deer's face looked strange and frightening to the young deer. The young buck couldn't see it clearly, but the old buck had only one eye in his head, and one empty socket. The one eye stared across the pond. The empty socket also seemed to stare. The young buck felt afraid. His legs began to quiver. He slowly backed out of the water, then turned and retreated into the woods. Once in the cover of the trees, he looked back across the pond. The one-eyed buck was gone.

At nightfall the clearing came alive with the chirping of crickets in the grasses and the plunking banjo-like calls of green frogs in the pond. A pair of little brown bats swooped down out of a pondside tree rapidly flapping their skin wings, flying low over the water after emerging black flies and mosquitoes. The beavers left their lodge and swam close together out on the pond, their widening V-shaped wakes blending and rippling behind them. Somewhere in the darkening woods a barred owl hooted eight notes.

The buck and doe were feeding on blackberry leaves in a copse a hundred feet upstream from where the brook entered the thicket. The twins both had their heads deep in the bushes when, without a sound, two new deer entered the small clearing. They were yearlings also, both does, reared by an old woodland doe who was now nursing new fawns. One of the twin does had a patch of white hair about the size of a maple leaf marking her right shoulder. Otherwise they were nearly identical. Together they eased into the center of the copse and sidled up to the buck and doe, both of whom snapped up tall and alert.

After a brief period of nervous foot stomping, sniffing, and snorting, each pair of twins accepted the other. While the buck behaved as he always had, independent and somewhat aloof, the company of the new deer had a profound effect on his sister. Almost instantly, she felt less fearful. Although her instinct for danger was still as sharp as ever, in the small herd she felt more safe and secure.

The four deer fed on and off in the copse until dawn and then into the morning. When the moon was a faint chalky face in blue sky, and the sun was beginning to shine into the copse, the deer bedded down right where they were. The three does lay close together amid the tangle of blackberry stems, the buck some distance away near the brook. He felt a slight itching in one of his antlers and reached his long neck back to rub the velveted spike against his side. Then he rested his chin on his outstretched foreleg and dozed off.

The does were too alert to sleep. They spent the remaining morning hours getting acquainted —looking one another over, and listening to one another's calm and assuring munching sounds as they chewed their cuds.

In the middle of the afternoon, the does arose and began to feed again, nibbling their way around

the small clearing. The buck awakened but remained bedded down. He could hear the three
does feeding. A swallowtail butterfly winged into
the copse and alighted on a small sunlit pile of
pine needles near him. He observed the butterfly
as it flexed its large black wings slowly down, then
slowly up. Down, slowly, then up. Down. Up.
The slow movements were hypnotic, and the buck
fell into a deep sleep.

The sun was low and the copse completely

shaded when the buck finally awoke. He listened for the does but heard no sounds of their footsteps or feeding. He stood and stretched and looked around. No does. He walked around the copse, searching for his sister and her new companions, and found their fresh trail leading away into the woods. But rather than follow, the buck remained in the copse, a bit unsure of what to do. His antlers itched again, and again he reached back and rubbed them on his flank.

Once more, the buck sniffed the hoofprints in the does' departing trail. Then he turned away from the scent and took his first steps toward solitary ways.

CHAPTER FIVE

*T*he weeks went by. Summer, green and lush, ripened and then drew to a close. As the hours of daylight slowly began to decrease, the deer gradually shed their red-brown hairs and changed to warmer blue-gray winter coats. They fed for longer periods of time, harvesting summer's bounty, building up reserves of fat for the coming colder months.

The three yearling does joined the old woodland doe and her fast-growing fawns, and the group moved upriver to the meadow. There they banded with another small group of does, a few of them with summer fawns.

Though the young buck still visited the beaver pond, he spent less time there and more time ranging through the woodland. Living alone was making him more wary. He no longer had his sister's constant vigilance to warn him of approaching danger. He became less active in the daylight hours, bedding earlier and arising later, often after dark, to feed. His antlers, now fully grown, were hardening inside the velvet. The velvet was drying up and had begun to peel, revealing the sharp points of two long spikes.

Though the young buck chose to wander and bed alone, he sought out many of the same feeding and drinking places frequented by the does and fawns and by other solitary bucks. He followed the deer trails, arriving to eat or drink just after the other deer had gone.

One warm September night, after following a long and winding deer trail around a wooded hill, the young buck happened into a secluded stand of evergreens. Moonlight streamed down through the trees. The ground was carpeted with club moss and sprinkled with fallen needles. The buck's hooves pressed deeply and silently into the softness. He paused to sniff the still air and sample it for warning scents. But the pleasant fragrances of pine and spruce and hemlock were all he smelled. Suddenly he noticed two shining dots of light in a darkened cluster of small evergreens, just off the trail some fifty feet ahead. The buck stared at the bright dots, concentrating on the shadowed shape around them, until he could make out the silhouetted head and shoulders of an animal crouched low against the ground.

The bobcat had been hiding motionless amid the small trees for some time, watching the trail, waiting for a hare to hop by. The deer was far bigger game, something the bobcat was hesitant to tackle.

In his mind, the buck could not connect the glowing eyes and shadowy shape, both so low to the ground, with any animal he had seen before. Curious, he took a few steps forward. The bobcat cringed backward in his tracks and partially un sheathed his claws.

Seeing the slow shrinking motion sent a shiver through the deer. He felt the muscles in his legs tighten. His thinking process stalled and became paralyzed with uncertainty. All he could do was stare, unblinking, at the figure in the shadows.

The bobcat, emboldened by the deer's inaction,

pressed forward on the mossy ground and slowly allowed the full length of his claws to emerge. They glinted in the moonlight. In a flash of recognition, the buck linked the creature he was facing with his memory of the low and slinking shape of the bobcat he had seen before, prowling in the thicket. Fear began to mount inside him. He felt the urge to run.

Just then, deep in the silent, windless forest, a ripe old rotted tree trunk cracked and came crashing down. The buck took off. So did the bobcat, in the opposite direction.

The remainder of September passed by quickly. The buck did little more than eat and rest and move on, always following the freshest trail of the does. He did not see the bobcat again, but he often came upon its tracks and scent.

One late September night, he heard coyotes howling at the moon. Even though they sounded far away, their weird chaotic chorus sent a chill down his spine and raised the hairs on the nape of his neck. Twice in his solitary travels, he saw the one-eyed buck—once at a great distance and once quite close, across a deep ravine. But in the time since their first encounter at the beaver pond, the young buck had grown in weight and stature, and each of his subsequent sightings of the fierce-looking older buck left a less disturbing impression in his mind.

As the season changed, the buck, too, was undergoing changes, becoming sexually mature. By mid-October, after months of solitude, he longed for company—but not that of other bucks. His mind dwelled on recalled images of does. He was experiencing the first stages of the rut—the mating season for deer, which comes every autumn. The young buck began to sense a pressure building inside him. It made him irritable, and at times when the pressure was unbearable, he lashed out, stabbing his peeling antlers at saplings or brush. Gradually, from hormonal flow and the building of muscle from the exercise of sparring with young trees, the buck's neck swelled. The remaining velvet on his now bone-hard antlers was mostly dried up, and it itched and tickled, hanging down against his head. To alleviate the feeling, he rubbed his antlers against the stem and branches of a small but resilient cinnamon birch tree for two whole nights, until every bit of the annoying velvet, and much of the young tree's bark, had been scraped away. Finally bared, the buck's long, perfectly symmetrical antlers gleamed—two long spikes, smeared reddish-brown from blood left in the last of the drying velvet, to crown him at the onset of his first rutting season.

A buck's antlers are what makes him unique. The size and shape and breadth from point to point of Long Spikes' antlers were different from those of any other buck's antlers, even other bucks with only first-year spikes. Though now the highly sensitive velvet was gone and the antlers themselves had no nerve endings, Long Spikes nevertheless could feel them on his forehead. And from his extraordinary memory of them growing, he knew exactly how long each spike was. With two long sharp weapons to fight off any other buck that might get in his way, he trailed the does, no longer looking for their feeding places and drinking spots, but for the does themselves.

CHAPTER SIX

*W*hile all the sexually mature bucks were feeling strong mating urges, the does were not yet ready to mate. And unlike the bucks who all entered the rut around the same time, each individual doe would be ready only at her time of estrus—the one or two day period within a doe's reproductive cycle when she is capable of becoming pregnant. For many in the herd, such a time was weeks away. A yearling doe's first period of estrus marks her coming of age. The white-patched doe, her twin, and Long Spikes' sister were undergoing subtle changes inside their bodies, but they looked and behaved the same as always. They were still a closely knit trio, feeding and drinking, playing and bedding together as they followed the herd from meadow to river to woodland to bog. But now they traveled at a quicker pace, in order to keep ahead of the pursuing males.

Long Spikes was so intent on finding the does that he forgot to eat, and bedded only when he became exhausted. When he happened on a fresh doe trail, he'd walk briskly along, nose to the ground, ignoring anything and everything but the tracks before him. He became unwary, even reckless. No longer did he travel only under the cover of darkness. He tracked the does in broad daylight.

So far all the trails Long Spikes followed led to places where the does had recently been but no longer were. He grew increasingly frustrated. As he sank deeper into his rut, his frustration grew into anger and he took it out on tender young trees—lunging repeatedly at a tree stem as if he were fighting an opponent.

Late one morning, while searching for hoof prints on the riverbank, Long Spikes came upon a deer trail so fresh that he snapped up tall and looked ahead, expecting to see the does. A heavy morning fog was still hanging in the air, and was only very slowly being burned away by the sun. Long Spikes followed the trail, the scent lingering on every grass blade and leaf the does had brushed against, and hanging like a perfumed curtain in the microscopic water globules of mist suspended in the air above the trail.

Long Spikes walked briskly, his nose poked way out ahead, his tail held up stiffly. When the trail made a wide half circle around the white house of the farmer who owned the land along the river, and skirted the farmer's big red barn, Long Spikes hardly noticed either house or barn.

A large golden retriever was sleeping in the hazy sunlight on the well-worn floorboards at the barn entrance. Like all farm dogs, he was not chained or tied, but allowed to roam freely around the house and barn. His roving presence kept the coyotes from coming near the livestock. He was an active watchdog, ever patrolling the corn for crows and raccoons, and chasing rabbits and woodchucks from the garden. Because he was a hunting breed, he instinctively flushed wild birds, and occasionally tracked deer, but so far hadn't caught up with one. Now when the big dog was suddenly awakened by Long Spikes' scent drifting slowly on the mist, he traced the drifting scent to the fresh trail on the outskirts of the farmyard and followed.

The does' trail led Long Spikes to a lone old apple tree at the meadow edge. The does and fawns had stopped here to feed on windfalls before going out into the field to graze. Long Spikes sniffed the ground and the half-eaten apples all around the tree. Then he spotted one doe far out on the field in the mist. As he looked, another doe appeared, then another. Like ghostly apparitions the grazing does and fawns faded in and out of sight as they moved, slowly stepping, nibbling off the tender tips of grass and the sweetest leaves of clover.

Long Spikes fixed his eyes on the dream-like vision of one doe and was starting toward her when he heard thumping on the ground behind him. He spun around and saw the dog galloping toward him through the fog. Long Spikes snorted in alarm and took off across the meadow, heading for the wooded hill and away from the grazing does.

Out on the grass the white-patched doe was the first to spot the running buck and the smaller form of the dog running behind. She stomped a forefoot, sending warning vibrations to the other deer. Then she fled, her white tail raised high. Instantly, all the other deer bounded off, scattering at first, then regrouping as they drew nearer to the river on the far side of the meadow.

Long Spikes sprinted to the foot of the wooded hill. As he leaped the old stone wall, his left hind foot became momentarily snared in a loop of ancient barbed wire, halting him abruptly in midair and bringing him down on his side with a heavy thud. As Long Spikes was getting to his feet, the dog, unaware that the deer was just beyond the wall, leaped over it himself. The shocked retriever collided with the buck. Long Spikes did not use his antlers. He kicked out with his front legs, one razor-edged hoof cutting a gash in the dog's forehead. Yelping and growling, the dog scrambled out from under the buck and ran away.

Long Spikes ran up the wooded slope and trotted along the ridge. Then, turning on a well-worn path, he headed for the alder thicket.

The morning sun had burned off all the fog by the time Long Spikes waded into the beaver pond and bathed his ankle wound in the cool clear water. He had left the dog far behind, and for the moment, the does were far from his mind. A kingfisher flew chattering overhead. Long Spikes took a long drink, then bedded for the day in the tall grasses near the water.

CHAPTER SEVEN

*T*he last days of October were crisp and cool and brilliant. The does and fawns kept moving, but avoiding the rutting bucks was becoming more and more difficult. Many more bucks, each following the mating urge and his nose, had migrated to the area. Bucks Long Spikes' age with first-year spikes; two-and-a-half-year-olds with "forked," four-pointed antlers of their second rutting season; and older bucks, veterans of many ruts, with imposing racks of six, eight, ten, and even twelve long, sharply pointed antler tines—all were traveling the same worn paths. Their signs were everywhere: slender tree stems rubbed barkless by bucks polishing their antlers; saplings torn apart by bucks venting their frustration at being unable to locate the elusive does. The bigger bucks created oval "scrapes" in the ground where in rage they pivoted around, pawing with their front hooves. Having made such a scrape, a buck marked the spot with urine and then moved on. When one buck came upon another's scrape, he too would become enraged and take his turn at the same spot, pawing at and urinating on the scraped ground.

When two bucks met face to face, the confrontation often led to combat. Throughout the woodland, the rattling of antlers engaged in battle became a familiar sound. Most of the fights were between bucks of equal size and stature. Young bucks with small antlers tended to back down from confrontations with bigger, more experienced, heavily antlered bucks.

Long Spikes had not yet had any opportunity to take part in a fight, or to back down from one. He had not even witnessed any fights between bucks. Then, early one November morning when the leaves were mostly gone from the trees, he happened on a pair of bucks squaring off near the rim of a large gully in a grove of maple trees. The two deer were not much bigger than Long Spikes, but each had a fairly large set of antlers—one buck with six points, the other with an uneven rack of five.

From behind a smooth maple trunk, Long Spikes watched as the deer faced off, each with his ears pressed back in aggression. Long Spikes flinched as the two bucks charged each other, hooking their antlers together, tangling head to head. The six-pointer pushed powerfully, forcing the five-pointer to hold his ground by digging his sharp-edged hooves into the leafy soil. For a few moments it was a standoff. Then, lunging forward, the five-point buck forced his opponent backward, and kept forcing until the buck tumbled over. Quickly the dominant fighter disentangled his antlers from his opponent's and stabbed two of his five points into the fallen deer's shoulder. Blood oozed from the wounds. Again the five-point buck slashed forward, but the bleeding deer had regained his footing and avoided being stabbed.

In close quarters, the deer charged again. This time their antlers collided with such tremendous force that they locked together. The battle went on as the bucks shoved and pushed each other around, each using his powerful neck to shake his head, trying to break free. One buck stumbled and fell, bringing his adversary down with him. They rolled, one over the other, heads locked together, down into the gully, and lying at the bottom still locked head to head, continued fighting.

Long Spikes moved closer to see down into the gully. The bucks below were grunting and snorting, flailing their legs, violently kicking the air in an effort to get up. But when one even began to get footing, the other's jerking and kicking pulled him back down. Then all of a sudden both deer stopped and lay still on the ground, their tongues hanging out from exhaustion, their sides heaving great breaths. Long Spikes approached the gully rim and walked all around it, looking down at the deer. He was at once frightened and fascinated. He stood on the rim and pawed at the ground, knocking loose bits of earth and small pebbles down onto the motionless deer. Then Long Spikes snorted loudly and the sound reanimated the two fighting bucks. Instantly both deer kicked out wildly, and finally twisting together in just the right way, they stood.

Long Spikes shrank back away from the rim and took cover again behind a tree as the two bucks jerked each other up out of the gully. Then, by wrenching their necks from side to side with combined bursts of great strength, they broke free. Slowly, cautiously, the deer backed off and away. The fight was over. Neither buck had won.

For the next few days Long Spikes behaved as though he had been the victor in the terrible gully battle. Highly stimulated by what he had witnessed, he pranced around, snorting, and waged a private war on a slender striped maple.

The turned-on young buck lunged repeatedly at the resilient little tree. He hooked his long spikes around the tree's smooth stem and rubbed hard against it, scraping off bark as he did so. His antlers, bleached by sunlight to a very light tan, were being polished to a satiny luster by the constant rubbing. Long Spikes charged the tree again and rattled his antlers against the thin branches. He snorted and grunted. Something grunted back. Long Spikes froze still at the sound. The thing grunted again.

Long Spikes pulled back from the tortured tree
and saw the one-eyed buck standing just a dozen
feet away, facing him head-on. For the first time,
the two were together in close quarters, and Long
Spikes could clearly see the big deer. The old buck
did not stand very tall, but he was long bodied
and barrel chested. The base of his muscular neck

was as big around as Long Spikes' midsection. The bigger deer's antlers had heavy main beams, and each of his ten antler tines was as thick and long and sharply pointed as the younger buck's spikes. And there was the empty eye socket, the eyeball plucked out in a fight long ago by a poking antler point, the socket dark and sunken and scarred around.

A gust of wind combed through the tree tops, loosing a few autumn leaves. The colorful leaves sailed downward on the air between the bucks, their graceful twirling motions capturing some tiny portion of each deer's attention. As the leaves settled to the ground, the old buck's ears pressed back tight against his head. He flared his nostrils and snorted a challenging cloud of steam into the cold air. Then slowly, steadily, he swaggered forward, his body broadside to his opponent. Long Spikes stood trembling, frozen with fear. When the older buck's one fierce eye was less than a yard away from Long Spikes' two, the big deer lunged, swiftly slashing his massive antlers at Long Spikes' head. Long Spikes ducked, dropping down on his front knees. He rolled over, then gathered his legs beneath him and escaped into the woods.

It was a night of northern lights. To the west the sky turned bright red. The southern sky turned green. In the other quadrants, streaks of pink and white reached upward waving, blending, until the whole sky was pulsating with the glowing light. Stars twinkled through the colors.

The lights in the sky shone into the woodland, creating tree shadows that moved as the lights moved. Long Spikes imagined every moving shadow was the one-eyed buck coming again to fight him. He spun around to face each new dark shape, and pawed the glowing ground with his hooves. Amid the restless shadows, Long Spikes saw the forms of three deer moving silently between the trees. They veered and soon were upwind of the watching buck. Long Spikes caught the scent of doe—more urgently, the scent of doe in estrus. He raised his head high and curled his upper lip excitedly. Then he made his move.

It was the lead doe who was in estrus. When she heard and saw the buck coming, she stopped, and letting her companions pass, she waited for him.

Long Spikes approached and sniffed the doe's hindquarters. As the doe walked round slowly, rays of northern lights played on her neck and back, illuminating the distinctive white patch on her shoulder. Long Spikes did not recognize the white-patched doe, nor did he realize that one of her two companions was his twin. He was completely engrossed in the moment. He walked closely beside the doe. The two deer circled twice in the shifting light. Then Long Spikes backed off to the doe's hind end and, mounting, covered her.

Though the coupling lasted but a few seconds, the process of new life had begun.

The doe stayed with Long Spikes for the remainder of the night, walking by his side, feeding, and coupling a few more times. Then, when the northern lights began to fade and the first pale yellow glow of morning dawned, she left to find the other does. Long Spikes didn't follow. Instead he bedded on a ridge alone just as the sun came up.

CHAPTER EIGHT

November's first real blast of frigid north-west winds whipped the long branches of hardwood trees and stripped from them their last clinging leaves. Still waters began to ice over. A dusting of snow covered the ground, which was freezing fast.

The sudden bitter weather forced a change in the deer's movements. They kept more to sheltered areas, and fed in the open only when the wind died down. Though mating still continued among the herd, Long Spikes' rutting urge was rapidly abating. He spent more time feeding. He ranged the woods in search of acorns.

One cold and cloudy morning, after a long night of feeding on fallen acorns beneath a massive oak, Long Spikes felt an impulse to return to the alder thicket, which was close by. There beside the frozen beaver pond, he plopped down on his full belly and soaked up what little sun there was. His hip bone poking up beneath his coat showed just how gaunt he had become while he was in the rut. But his health was sound and he was regaining weight. His coat was rich and full and steely gray in color. His antler spikes were bleached pure white—as white as the powdery snow he lay upon.

Just as more snow began to fall, a thumping noise out on the pond alerted Long Spikes. He stared at the spot on the ice where the noise seemed to be coming from.

Under the frozen surface of the pond, the male beaver had left the lodge by way of an underwater tunnel. He was attempting to come to shore so he could cut and gather more twigs to increase his winter stores, but he had found himself locked in by thin but solid ice. Repeatedly, the beaver banged the underside of the ice with the broad hard dome of his forehead, trying to break through. He had no fear of drowning. He had plenty of air in his lungs, and he could always swim back through the tunnel and up into the lodge's air-filled chamber to breathe. Crack! He bumped the undersurface of the frozen pond again, and this time he broke through. Out popped the beaver's wet head with a pane of thin broken ice balancing comically on top. The beaver looked all around. He then laboriously climbed out onto the slippery surface of the pond.

Long Spikes had been fascinated by the beaver ever since the first night he saw him feeding on the brook bank. Now, Long Spikes watched as the beaver crawled slowly on his belly across the frozen pond, the thin ice giving and sinking slightly under his weight. Digging his front claws into the ice, the beaver pulled himself along, his hind legs barely helping in the effort, his wide, flat tail dragging. There was a creaking sound, and the ice collapsed beneath the beaver, plunging him back down into the black water.

Long Spikes watched the hole and waited for the beaver to emerge again. The snow fell more heavily. The air turned much colder. The beaver did not reemerge. He had gone back to the lodge, stopping first to pull two food twigs from an underwater storage pile. One stick was for him, the other for his mate.

Long Spikes stared a while longer at the broken black hole in the pond, and through the snow dotted air saw the hole mend over in a thin sheet of new ice. The snowflakes, large and slow falling, heaped upon the ground. The deer watched them landing on the ice, on the dry grasses, on his coat. A great twirling cluster of snowflakes alighted on his nose, and licking his long tongue out, Long Spikes tasted and melted the cold crystals.

He swiveled his ears, cupping them in various directions, checking the thicket and the woods for sounds. All was silent. He turned his head slowly, surveying the scene for movements other than that of falling snow. And when he saw that the sky, the air, the ice, the trees, and the land were still, Long Spikes rested his chin on his shoulder and slept.

It was still snowing when daylight began to wane. Long Spikes felt hungry but was loath to leave his comfortable snow bed. A white hare hopped by, camouflaged against the snow. Long

Spikes heard the thumping of the hare's feet and saw the fresh tracks as they appeared, but he never saw the hare. A large female great horned owl, dark against the snowy landscape, swooped down from the woods into the thicket. Long Spikes saw the huge bird flying over and felt the soft swoosh of wings as they pumped the air above his head. The owl flew just beyond the nearby brush and then dropped like a stone out of sight. There was a high-pitched shriek. The owl flapped back up into the falling snowflakes and flew away with the white hare clutched in her talons.

Long Spikes rose to his feet and arched his back, stretching and flexing fully rested muscles. He walked to the pond edge, where the ice was so fragile it was transparent. He tapped the thin ice with his hoof, breaking a small hole, and drank through it. Then he turned and went into the snowy woods, heading for a place where he knew sweet birches grew.

He was passing by a tall, straight spruce tree when a faint, strange scent made him stop. Long Spikes raised his nose into the air. The wet snowflakes blotted out most smells, but enough of the strange odor was drifting between the flakes for Long Spikes to be sure it was not of the woods. He pressed closely against the straight spruce trunk. Then, ever so slowly, he stuck his long neck out and peeked in the direction of the odor. He saw a man raise his arms. Long Spikes ran. Bang! Pwtang! Something hard hit Long Spikes' right antler, shearing it off just above the base. Long Spikes ran faster. Bang! Another shot whizzed by his ear. In seconds the running deer put a great distance between himself and the man.

From the safety of cover behind a bushy white pine, Long Spikes looked back. The hunter walked up to the spruce tree and searched around the ground. Then, stooping, he picked an object off the snow and held it up to look it over. Long Spikes could not make out what it was. He felt pain on the right side of his forehead. The pedicel, where the broken antler base still was joined, was throbbing.

The hunter stood tall and put Long Spikes' broken antler in a pocket of his heavy coat. He straightened his hat, which had been knocked askew when he so quickly and excitedly raised his gun to shoot. He stared long in the direction of the deer's tracks and saw that they were rapidly filling in with snow. Then he turned and walked away.

By the next day the woods had become a dangerous, unpredictable place. The air was heavy with the scents of oiled metal, varnished wood, man, and tobacco. Even places the hunters' scents did not reach were not safe from stray bullets, which after missing their marks traveled for hundreds of yards before aimlessly striking trees, ricocheting off boulders, or simply landing with a hot, smoky thunk in the snow.

Long Spikes stayed high on a ridge where many trees had been logged off and there were plenty of sprout-covered stumps and slash piles of leftover branches and limbs to hide behind. But even with excellent cover, he was extra wary. Danger was everywhere.

Besides the new and overwhelming threat of the hunters, an old and familiar threat had returned. The coyotes had left the wilderness areas where they had been hunting all summer, and were back roaming the woodlands and fields, drawn by the slaughtering of deer. The coyotes too were at risk in a woods full of hunters and were being extra careful to stay out of sight. Like shadows in the forest they moved from tree to tree, from boulder to brush, sniffing around for the spoils of the hunt. As he stealthily moved around, Long Spikes did not see the coyotes, but he smelled them. And at night he could hear them, lapping deer blood off the snow and feasting on deer entrails the hunters discarded when butchering their kills.

After a week, Long Spikes began to feel the strain of the unrelenting danger. Every minute of daylight seemed more oppressive than the last, and each hour of darkness, haunted by the lingering scents of men and the sounds and scents of scavenging coyotes, was nightmarishly long. He laid low every day, all day. At night he walked in a frightened crouch, visiting feeding spots briefly, munching all he could, then slipping back into hiding to rechew it all in a cud.

One day just before dusk, Long Spikes was lying behind a large dump of logging slash, his head down, his one remaining antler blending in with the twigs poking up in the pile, when he heard men coming close by. Watching between the criss-crossing branches and limbs, he saw two hunters struggling to drag an extra heavy kill. Working in unison, heaving together, the men pulled the dead weight slowly over ten yards of the snow-covered ground. Then they rested, one standing, the other sitting on the hard rump of the deer. They talked quietly to each other. One of the men lit a cigarette. Tobacco smoke drifted to Long Spikes and he wrinkled his nose at the acrid smell.

All Long Spikes could see of the dead deer was its dark hind quarters and part of its white belly. The belly was cut open and the white hairs smeared with blood, the odor of which made Long Spikes feel sick. Without moving a muscle, not even to blink, he focused his eyes sharply on the bloody opening and saw nothing inside but rib-cage.

The hunters resumed dragging the deer, this time lifting the head and neck high to pull the body up over a log. Long Spikes finally saw the deer's face. It was the one-eyed buck! Long Spikes recognized the magnificent ten-point rack. The buck's one eye glared lifelessly. The missing eye's socket was an eerie white blank, packed full of snow.

CHAPTER NINE

*O*n a high treeless knoll, the hook-toothed
coyote sat tall on her haunches watching
the dawn. It had been another long night of
scavenging, but the findings were meager. During
the past few weeks she had gotten used to the
taste of deer blood and deer flesh, and she was
hungry for more. A small gastric storm rumbled
through her empty belly. She yawned a long yawn,
gaping her mouth wide and rolling her pink
tongue out into the air. She was with her mate,
a dark male, who was curled on the snow nearby,
catching a nap. Four offspring, one two-year-old
and three nearly fully grown seven-month-olds,
were sprawled around, quietly taunting one another, snapping their jaws against the snow, and
nipping at one another's fur.

As she had done for the past fourteen mornings,
the mother coyote listened carefully for the sounds

of hunters coming into the woods. But this morning she heard none.

One of the young coyotes stretched out on the snow, and reaching, bit his sister's ear, causing her to yelp loudly. The mother turned and glared at the two. The bickering stopped.

A soft wind was blowing up the ridge to the knoll. The old coyote sniffed to her left, straight ahead, and then to her right, checking the air for the scent of man. But the woods smelled only of trees and earth, water and snow, and wild creatures. The coyote picked up the faint scent of a deer and walked off the knoll toward it. One by one her family got up and followed.

Long Spikes was walking on a trail, in the morning light. The hunting had stopped and he knew it. All the tension that two weeks of hiding had built up inside him was suddenly, completely relieved. He stepped along, head high, flicking his tail, enjoying the fearless feeling.

A band of bluejays discovered a hornet nest in the top of a beech tree. The noisy birds flew close around the nest, picking at the delicate layers of paper, tearing them away to reveal the circular sections of comb inside. Then, in a frenzy, the bluejays ate all the frozen eggs and pupae and dead hornets remaining in the nest chamber. As the bluejays fed, large shreds of paper comb and nest wall wafted down and landed in a neat pile on the snowy ground. Long Spikes stepped up to the pile and inhaled its moldy aroma. Then, using his snout as a shovel, he playfully scooped the papery nest material high into the air and stood watching as the pieces floated around him back down to the ground.

A cold wind blew through the woods, whisking the nest pieces off the ground and sending them whirling away. The wind in the woods grew stronger. The air was bitterly cold. Long Spikes followed the trail into a small hollow, thickly grown from slope to slope with juniper bushes and small cedar trees. There, protected from the wind by the dense evergreen foliage, he nipped spicy cedar greens and nibbled tart juniper needles.

High above the hollow, a crow was flapping its wings in the cold air, trying hard to fly against the wind. Finding a pocket of calm under a gust, the crow ducked into it and sailed easily for a ways. Then abruptly, the crow somersaulted in flight and dive-bombed toward the cedars, calling out "Ca-ca-caw-ca-ca-caw-caw-caw." The bird hovered just above the tops of the small trees, screaming wildly. Long Spikes was alert, tracking the crow's noisy progress. Whatever the crow was railing at was heading toward Long Spikes.

Heeding the warning, the buck took off running, brushing against the closely spaced trees as he ran. Behind him he heard footfalls and the sounds of twigs snapping and branches being swooshed aside. He gathered speed and ran as fast as he could, pushing through the tight spaces between the cedar trees and leaping over squat juniper bushes. The sounds behind him became louder, the footfalls landed faster. Long Spikes heard the heavy breathing of large animals running hard. Now the crow was nearly overhead, still screaming frantically. Long Spikes charged through a last screen of cedars and bounded uphill out of the hollow.

Seconds later, the whole pack of coyotes, headed up by the hook-toothed female, burst out of the cedar woods.

Unsuccessful at summoning the flock, the crow, reacting violently to a natural enemy, dived at the pack, attacking the big dark male. Without breaking stride, the coyote snapped his jaws at the crow, plucking some tail feathers and flipping the squawking bird over in the air. Flapping wildly, the crow ascended and retreated back over the cedar tops, still calling out for reinforcements.

Long Spikes cleared a deadfall at full speed and

ran along the wooded ridge, ducking limbs and brittle twigs. As he ran he took great gulps of air. He was becoming overheated. A continuous cloud of steam issued from his back.

The coyotes spread out on the ridge, still behind but beginning to surround the running deer. Long Spikes turned abruptly to the right on a trail leading downhill off the hill's spine. As the coyotes all turned together, they fell back into ranks until they flowed like a plume of gray smoke in Long Spikes' direction.

At the bottom of the hill, Long Spikes turned again, this time to the left, into a thick growth of sumac. The coyotes made good time down the rocky hillside and were into the sumac on his heels. Long Spikes turned again, at full speed, to the right. He squeezed under a low sumac leaning over the trail, then turned again, to the left.

The coyotes collided and scrambled, trying to get by the low-hanging sumac all at once and stay hot on the trail of the maneuvering deer. Then Long Spikes abandoned his zigzagging course and took off like a shot across a long, flat, sparsely wooded plateau, heading toward the river, which he could hear but not see.

The coyotes started yapping and growling as they broke onto the plateau. Immediately they spread out, forming a broad bow. With few obstacles to slow them down, they closed in on their quarry.

Long Spikes was getting tired. He barely cleared a large boulder that lay in his way, his hind hooves scraping the stone. He saw the running shape of a dark coyote on his left. On his right, he saw two lighter-colored coyotes coming closer. Ahead, just over a rise, the river came into view. Just then he felt a nipping on his hind legs, and panic rose in him.

The mother coyote snapped her jaws and again nipped Long Spikes' running feet. The river was only twenty yards away. Long Spikes' ribs were heaving. His mouth was beginning to froth at the sides. His tongue was hanging out. The other coyotes were catching up, and as Long Spikes and the whole running pack reached the crest of the rise, the mother coyote lunged forward and bit into the tip of Long Spikes' tail, snagging more muscle than hair with her one hooked fang. Long Spikes felt the pain and leaped for his life, plunging into the river and pulling the coyote in with him.

The rest of the coyotes went berserk, leaping and climbing over one another on the snowy bank, stepping into the rushing stream and swimming a few feet, then paddling back out. Finally regaining composure, they all ran barking along the river-bank, following the action out in the water.

With the coyote still attached to his tail and the noisy pack of coyotes dogging him from the shore, Long Spikes swam as fast as he could, going with the current. His coat of hollow hairs kept him buoyant. As he swam, his kicking hind hooves pummeled the desperately paddling coyote's front legs and chest. She jerked her head in the water and pulled on the deer's tail, trying to rip free. But her hooked tooth held her fast.

Once the long outer hairs of the coyote's coat were thoroughly wetted, the cold river saturated the soft fuzzy undercoat next to her skin. Water-logged, her bushy tail became heavy and sank, pulling her hind end down with it. Long Spikes' torso began listing under the load. He kicked extra hard to keep himself upright, and his high-kicking hind hooves battered the coyote's neck, badly bruising her windpipe. The coyote flailed her limbs and splashed. She was gasping for air. Then, in a final effort to escape, she shook her head violently up and down, and at last she tore herself free. She swam weakly but steadily to shore and crawled up on the bank.

The other coyotes gave up the chase and ran back to the old female. Her fur was all stringy and wet. Worn and frustrated, she was in no mood to be crowded, and snarled at the bunch. A small clump of deer tail was still snagged on her fang.

Long Spikes headed across the current toward the bank farthest away from the coyotes. But there the stream was frozen and the water very deep. He tried to crawl out onto the frozen surface, but the ice kept breaking, plunging him back down. Splashing in the cold water, and kicking out with his front hooves, Long Spikes broke away ice, chopping his way forward a few inches at a time.

Then he rested, swimming in tight circles within the hole he had created.

Again he lunged forward, splashing in the water, kicking at the ice, and then rested. The next time Long Spikes lunged forward, he brought both fore-legs up high out of the stream and stomped down forcefully with both hooves, breaking whole chunks of the confining ice. It was an exhausting effort, and Long Spikes sank in the water, his eyes submerged, his nose breathing in a little water with air. He summoned strength, heaved upward and kicked at the ice again, and again, and again, until finally he was so close to the shore that he could see mouse tracks on the snow. He lunged forward once more, thrusting himself out of the water, and flopped onto the last few feet of ice. There the ice was much thicker and it held his weight.

Long Spikes lay still until he felt his wet body freezing to the ice. He crawled forward on his belly to the snowy bank. Then, shaking and shivering, soaked to the skin, he got up on his feet, staggered to a fallen log, and collapsed.

Long Spikes did not move for two whole days. The first day he lay shivering against the log. He consumed only snow. On the second day the weather was much milder. A couple of chickadees showed up. Their soft tweezling calls soothed Long Spikes' mind. The sun shone on Long Spikes. His coat revived. His skin dried. His muscles warmed. At sundown, he stood for the first time since he crawled out of the stream.

Long Spikes arched his back very slowly to stretch, and as he did he heard the faint popping and creaking of stiff muscles contracting and expanding. He wiggled his tail, now jagged at the end where the coyote had torn off the tip. The chickadees flitted through the brush on the bank. Long Spikes watched the tiny birds seek out and take bits of bark fungus into their beaks. Some of the fungus was on a tree branch close to Long Spikes. He nibbled a small piece and chewed. He ate some more.

CHAPTER TEN

*T*he riverbank with its cover of pines and the tender browse of small waterside birches was a good place for Long Spikes to stay and regain his strength. But it was a place he had never been to before, and would never have come to had he not been pursued by the coyotes. A little way at a time, he wandered back upstream, crossed the river at a safe place, and returned to his home range.

As he walked on his side of the river, Long Spikes was alert for the coyotes, but he neither heard, smelled, nor saw them. Though the coyotes had gone away, they were still present in his mind. The horrific close call haunted him. For days, while feeding or drinking—times when a deer is most vulnerable—Long Spikes would remember the coyotes chasing him, or the coyote biting into his tail, and a jolt of fear would run through him. He remembered the terrible swim in the ice cold river. Sometimes the images that flashed in his mind were so vivid, he would leave his feeding spot at once to hide.

December storms heaped snow on the woodland. One storm lasted a whole day and night, adding a foot and a half of fresh snow to the already deep layer on the ground. Just walking in such depth took a great deal of energy. Trailing out of their three-season areas, the deer herd began the long trek to their winter grounds, in a forest of evergreen trees where strong winds seldom blew and snow sifted gently down through the sheltering boughs. On the journey to the winter grounds, old does led their large families of young does and immature bucks. Mature bucks of various sizes and statures, now well beyond the rutting season and no longer competitive, traveled together in small bands. Some of the bucks had already shed their antlers.

Deer antlers are shed annually. When a deer's antlers are ready to shed, they simply drop off—sometimes both at once, most often one at a time. Long Spikes' broken right stub of an antler had fallen off somewhere without him noticing it. The pedicel, where the antler stub had been attached, and where next year a new and most likely forked antler would grow, was sore. With only a single long spike left, his forehead felt unbalanced. From time to time he shook his head, trying to rid himself of the lopsided feeling.

Each night when he traveled, Long Spikes walked through the deep snow at a slow steady pace, conserving his energy for the time when he might have to run from danger. As soon as the opportunity presented itself, he joined up with two other bucks—for the safe feeling of being one of a group instead of alone. Almost immediately his haunting memory of the coyotes faded. Long Spikes' new companions were older and bigger than he. One had recently shed both of his antlers. The other buck still carried his eight-point rack. The eight-pointer had a distinctive white patch on one of his legs, having come from the same line of deer as the white-patched doe Long Spikes had bred.

Night after night, the trio of bucks ambled along in the general direction of the winter grounds. Wherever they found abundant aspens or other favored food they lingered, sometimes for days.

There was no leader. Whenever one of the group moved on, the others went along. Early one morning, when they happened to be in the vicinity of the alder thicket, Long Spikes went to visit the beaver pond, and the two older bucks followed.

The sun was just coming up. Wide shafts of soft white light angled into the thicket. Long blue shadows of shoreline trees reached across the pond, accenting the dips and waves on the pond's thick snow blanket. Under the heavy snow, the pond ice moaned and creaked in flux. Long Spikes felt more at home at the pond than he did anywhere else. He looked around for familiar landmarks now buried in snow. On the dam where dark branches, sticks, and logs poked up out of the white, he saw snow crystals lying at right angles to the sunlight, sparkling and shining. The beavers' lodge was bare at the peak, where body heat from the beavers living inside escaped and melted away the snow.

The three bucks bedded on the pond bank, in deep soft snow. Long Spikes sank down near a clump of thin alder stems. Next to one alder stem a vole tunnel probed down into the luminous snow. Long Spikes fixed his eyes on the tiny blue-green hole and drifted in and out of sleep.

A sudden blast of wind-driven snow blew through the thicket. In the midst of the squall, a short caravan of does and summer fawns silently slipped by on the opposite side of the pond. In the procession were Long Spikes' sister, now pregnant, and the white-patched doe, who had inside her twin embryos Long Spikes had sired. The does moved purposefully along, eager to get to the evergreen woods and settle in for the rest of the winter.

Long Spikes' two companions noticed the doe caravan and rose to walk in the same direction. When Long Spikes stood up to follow, his one remaining antler dropped off his head and landed like a dagger, point-first in the snow. Surprised and uncertain, the buck looked closely at his shed spike. He sniffed the flat base and smelled his own scent on it. Still somewhat uneasy, but knowing he had to move on, he pranced backward, snorting a small cloud of breath into the cold snowy air. And after shaking his antlerless head a few times, he walked away to follow his kind.